starchasers

the galactic shopping mall

by

david orme

illustrated by
jorge mongioui

Ransom

starchasers

The Galactic Shopping Mall
by David Orme

Illustrated by Jorge Mongiovi

Published by Ransom Publishing Ltd.
Radley House, 8 St. Cross Road, Winchester, Hants. SO23 9HX, UK

www.ransom.co.uk

ISBN   978 184167 764 4

First published in 2009
Reprinted 2012, 2013

misha hanson

captain

- Owner of the *Lightspinner*.

- When her rich father died, Misha could have lived in luxury – but that was much too boring.

- She spent all the money on the *Lightspinner* – and a life of adventure!

- Misha is the boss – but she doesn't always get her own way.

"Whenever we're in trouble, I know I've got a great team with me. The Starchasers will never let me down!"

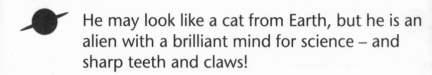

He may look like a cat from Earth, but he is an alien with a brilliant mind for science – and sharp teeth and claws!

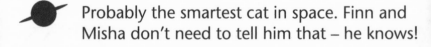

Probably the smartest cat in space. Finn and Misha don't need to tell him that – he knows!

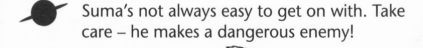

Suma's not always easy to get on with. Take care – he makes a dangerous enemy!

"Misha tells people I'm just a big softy. The biggest softy in the galaxy. You kno[w] what? She's wrong."

- Finn is a great guy to have around when there's trouble – and for the Starchasers, that's most of the time.

- Probably the best pilot Planet Earth has ever produced – though Misha and Suma don't tell him that, of course!

- Finn is great for getting the Starchasers out of (and sometimes in to) trouble! If only he didn't love gadgets so much …

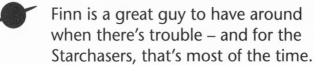

"I was in big trouble when Misha found me in an on-line computer game. She changed my life!"

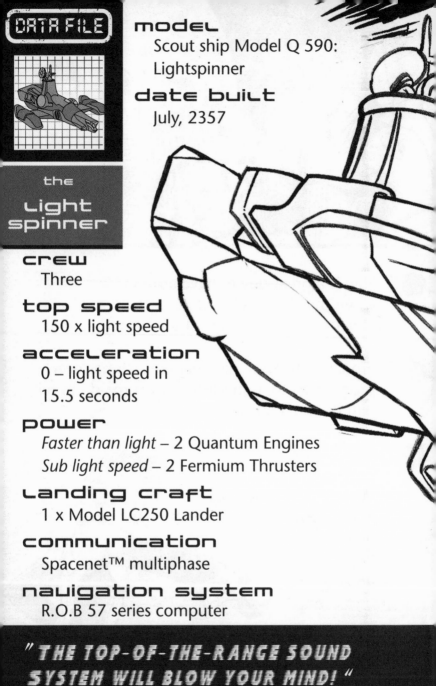

model
Scout ship Model Q 590:
Lightspinner

date built
July, 2357

the
Light spinner

crew
Three

top speed
150 x light speed

acceleration
0 – light speed in
15.5 seconds

power
Faster than light – 2 Quantum Engines
Sub light speed – 2 Fermium Thrusters

Landing craft
1 x Model LC250 Lander

communication
Spacenet™ multiphase

navigation system
R.O.B 57 series computer

"THE TOP-OF-THE-RANGE SOUND SYSTEM WILL BLOW YOUR MIND!"

"THE NEW Q590 – LIGHT SPEED IN 15.5 SECONDS – YOU'RE GONNA LOVE THIS BABY!"
WHAT SPACESHIP   JANUARY 2357

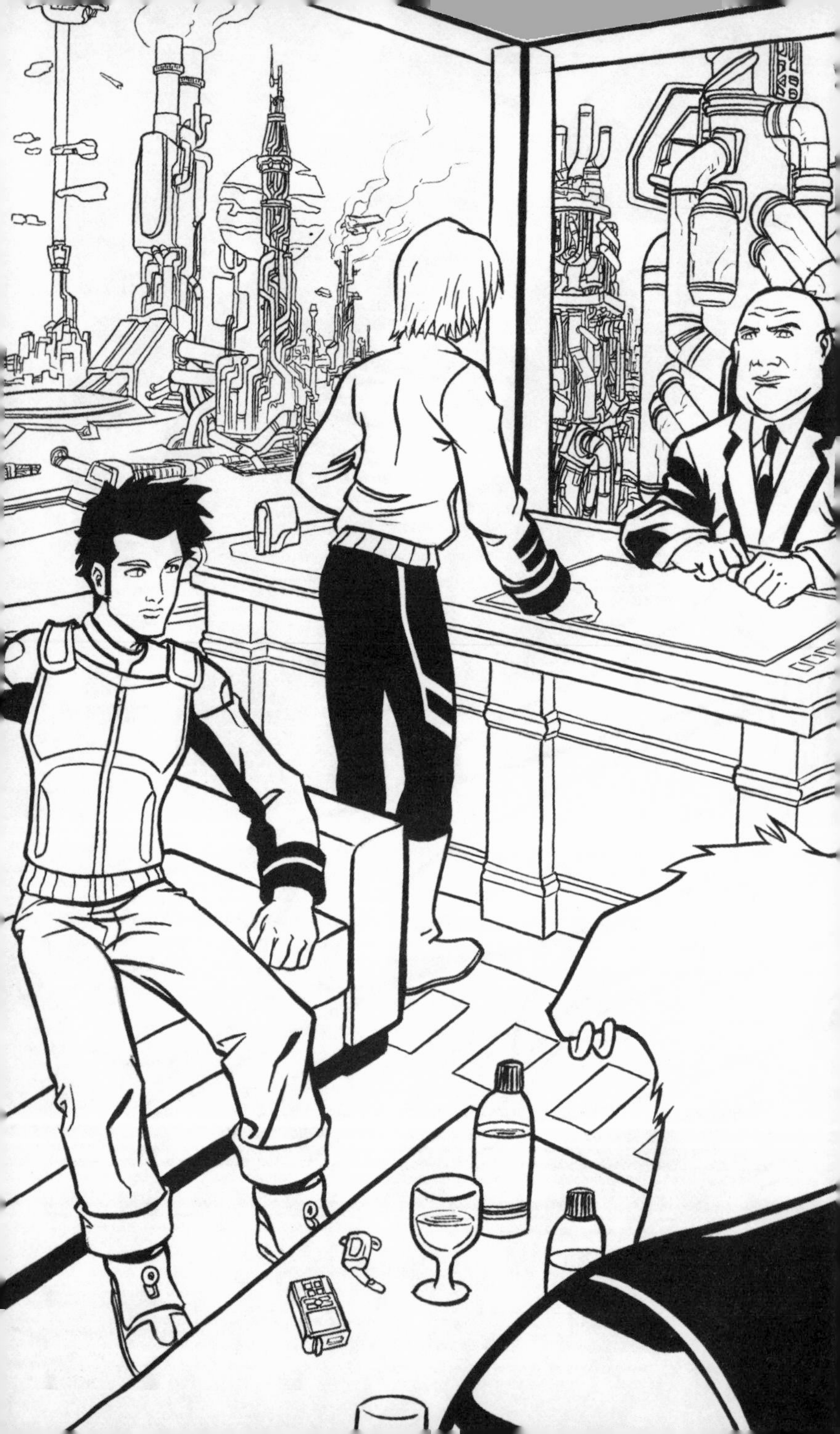

robocom inc.

The Starchasers had never been in an office as grand as this. Outside the window, the Robocom factory stretched for miles. Everything was huge – especially the boss, Ripp Gunn.

'So let's get this straight,' said Misha. 'You had a row with Ella, and now she's gone, and you'll pay us good money to find her?'

'That's right. Misha, you and Ella went to school together; she'll listen to you. It's vital that she comes back home soon.'

'Not sure it's any of our business,' said Finn. 'If Ella wants to go away for a while, surely that's up to her.'

'Yes, you're right, of course. But there's something else. I'm an old man, and I'm dying. Doctors tell me that in a couple of months I'll be dead. Ella's a good engineer and will take over the business. But I want to see her – talk to her – before it happens.'

'So what was the quarrel about?' asked Suma.

'I'm sorry, I can't tell you that.'

'Have you any idea where we should start looking?' asked Misha.

'Yes. I know exactly what planet she is on. And I'm afraid she is in great danger. She is on Trajan!'

trajan

'Trajan control. Identify.'

'Spaceship Lightspinner, with three crew.'

'Checking credit.'

There was silence for a few seconds.

'Credit O.K. Landing bay 59 – left.'

Misha and Suma looked down on to the planet's surface. It didn't look anything

special; mostly green fields growing food, with a food factory here and there, and eight spaceports scattered across the planet.

Finn smiled. There was much more to Trajan than you could see from space. The dangerous bit was underground.

It had all started a hundred years ago. A rich property dealer had bought land on the planet. He had a plan – to build the greatest shopping mall in the galaxy!

The shopping mall was a huge success. The galaxy was big, and many people earned lots of money. And people love shopping!

But people wanted choice, and soon more shopping malls appeared on Trajan. Because the weather was not good, the shopping malls were built underground.

More people came, and the shopping malls got bigger and bigger. Soon, the whole planet was nothing but tunnels, express railways, hotels, and of course, shops. Millions of them, all underground. People came for a shopping holiday and spent lots of money. Sometimes they just never went home.

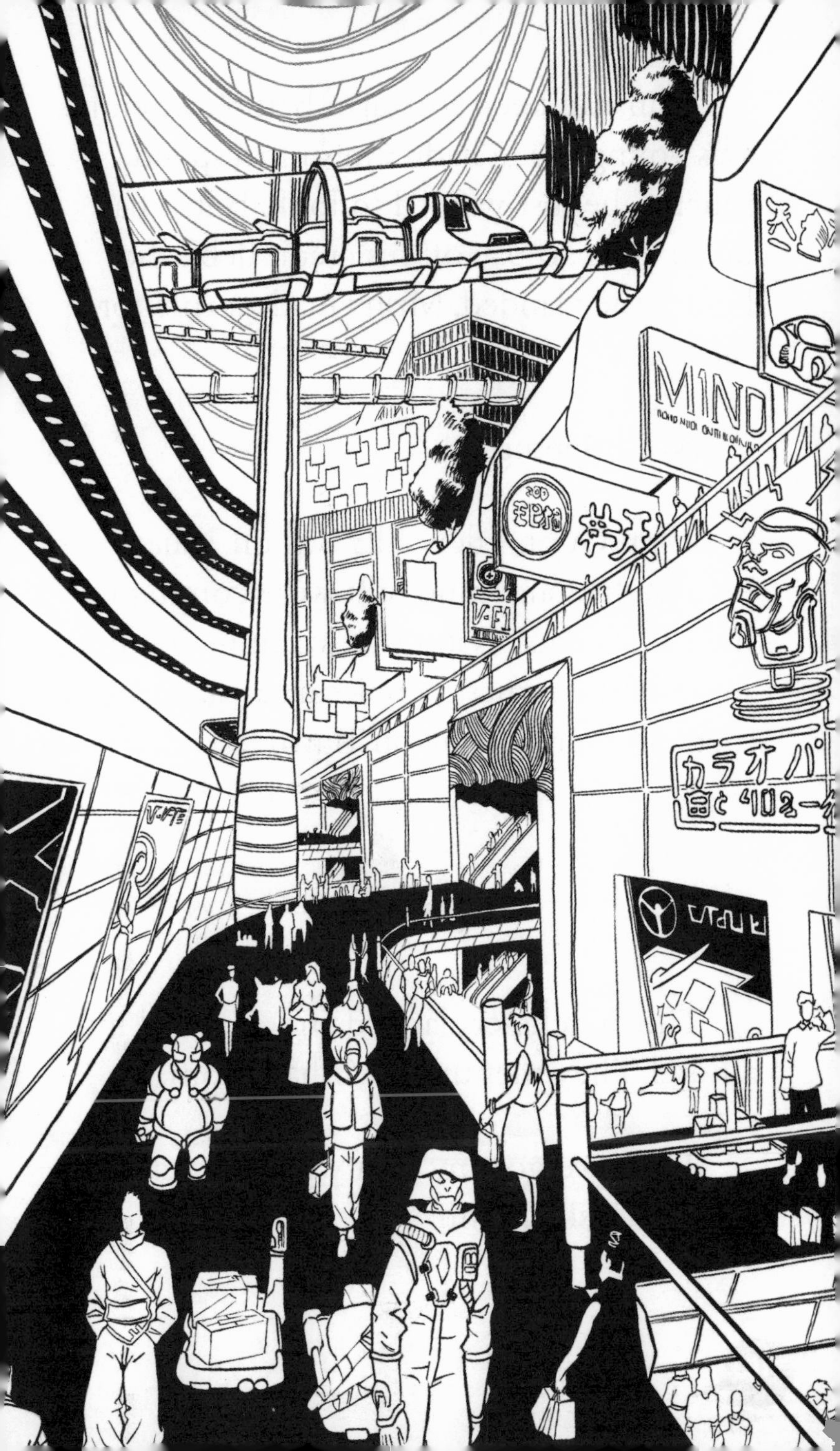
MIND
V-F1
カラオパ

Finn had been to Trajan before, when he was younger. He hadn't meant to spend much – he just wanted to look. But it had taken years to pay off his credit debts. So before they landed, Misha made a rule for the team.

No shopping!

Ripp Gunn knew Ella was on Trajan because her shopping bills were coming to him! Of course, Ripp was a rich man – but some of the richest people in the galaxy had spent all their money on Trajan.

The Starchasers landed and checked into a hotel. They met up in Misha's room.

'Have we got any idea where to start looking?' asked Finn.

'Not much,' said Misha. 'But we know she's been buying stuff in this part of the planet – we've got copies of the credit bills.'

'Let's head into the shops tomorrow and start checking the place out.'

'O.K.,' said Misha. 'I'm really worried that Ella has become a shopping addict. So remember what I said guys – no shopping!'

finn goes shopping

You could buy anything on Trajan.

Rare space diamonds? They had them. Works of art from aliens that had died out a million years ago? No problem. The very latest in handbags from Earth, made of solid gold, yet light as a feather to carry? Just step this way. Anything you could possibly want, though nothing you really needed.

And if you couldn't afford it, that was no problem – you could always get credit, even if your children and grandchildren would have to pay for it.

The Starchasers wandered on and on, deeper and deeper into the planet, until at last Suma had had enough. Everywhere there were shoppers: humans and aliens from every planet in the universe, all shopping!

It was all so easy. You didn't have to carry anything. All the things you bought would be delivered, gift-wrapped, to your hotel. After all, it wasn't real money, was it? Why not just keep on spending?

'I'm getting bored to death here! We've got a job to do. Remember?'

'Sorry, Suma,' said Misha. 'I was just looking at these great designer space boots ...'

'Well don't. And where's Finn?'

'Dunno. Think he may have gone in that gadget shop.'

'Oh no! Now we're in trouble.'

They went in the shop. A robot assistant was showing Finn the latest virtual world space helmet.

'Quick!' shouted Suma. 'He's about to pay for it! Grab him before it's too late!'

Finn was about to look into the machine that checked the pattern in his eye. No one had credit cards any more. They weren't safe.

But everyone's eye was different. That's how
you paid for things.

Suma and Misha grabbed Finn and
dragged him out of the shop. Three heavy
security robots tried to stop them, but
they got out just in time. Suma was really
annoyed with Finn.

'What were you doing in there, you
stupid Earth idiot! Did you see how much
that thing cost?'

'What thing?'

'That helmet!'

'What helmet?' Finn scratched his head. 'I don't remember … Oh, yes, wait a minute, I do!'

They walked past another branch of the same gadget shop, full of customers buying expensive stuff. Suma slipped a tiny machine out of his shoulder harness and looked at the screen.

'Thought so. They're using mind probes. Putting messages into your brain to make you buy things.'

'But that's against the law!' said Misha.

'Misha, this is Trajan. Remember what Ripp Gunn said. This place is dangerous!'

misha gets
a call

Just then Misha's spacephone bleeped. It was Ripp.

'Hi, Misha. Just had a report from Creditcom. Ella bought an ice-jewel necklace five minutes ago. You won't believe what it cost!'

Misha checked her Trajan shopfinder.

'That shop is only a kilometre away!
There's a flashcab over there. Get in – we
might just catch her!'

The flashcab raced down two levels, then dropped them off outside the jewellery shop. There was a dazzling display of ice diamonds in the widow. Only the richest people in the galaxy shopped here. Your credit was checked at the door. If you weren't loaded, you didn't get in.

'She'll have left by now. Any ideas?'

Misha thought. 'Maybe. Let's find the nearest food hall.'

Food was mostly free on Trajan – as long as you didn't stop shopping. The food shops checked how much you had spent before they served you. If you hadn't done enough shopping, you didn't get any food. You could get very hungry on Trajan.

All around the food hall were fast food places with food from everywhere in the galaxy. However alien you were, there was always something you would love to eat here. And it was FAST; they didn't want you to waste time eating when you could be shopping!

One of the places sold ice cream – the best in the galaxy. Misha knew Ella loved ice cream. And that's where they found her.

at the
hotel

'What do we do now?' whispered Finn. He loved ice cream too. If only they'd let him buy that helmet, he could have had some!

'We don't want to talk to her here,' said Misha. 'We need to find out where she's staying. She knows me, but she doesn't know you two. Follow her, then ring me.'

Misha disappeared. Ella finished her ice cream, then flagged down a flashcab. Suma and Finn jumped into another one.

'Follow that flashcab!'

At last Misha got a call from Suma.

'We followed her all afternoon. She spent enough money to buy a medium sized planet! How is it possible that a pair of shoes can cost more than a spaceship? Anyway, she gave up at last and headed to the Milton Hotel on level 8, sector 298. We're outside now.'

'Great work, guys. I'll be with you in ten minutes.'

The Trajan Milton Hotel had five thou-
sand rooms, and it would take months to
check them all. Luckily, not all the staff at the
hotel were robots. People staying there liked
real people to serve them. It was quite easy to
find people to work in the big hotels. They
were people that had spent all their money,
and had huge debts, and couldn't afford the
space fare home. They worked in the hotels
until they had enough money to get home.
Sometimes they died of old age first.

Finn found a hotel porter, a blue Nexian
from Sirius. He showed him a picture of Ella.

'Is this person staying at the hotel?'

'I'm sorry, I'm not allowed to tell you.'

'Here's a big wodge of cash, mate.'

'She's staying in room 4379.'

Misha knocked on the door of room 4379. There was no reply, but the door wasn't locked. The Starchasers pushed their way in.

Ella was sitting at her desk. She looked up.

'Misha! What are you doing here? And who are these people? What's going on?'

Suma's whiskers were twitching. His yellow eyes were staring at Ella. His whole body was tense.

Without warning, Suma leapt on to Ella, knocking her over. His teeth were at her throat.

‘Suma! What are you doing?’ Misha yelled, but Suma ignored her.

‘Now tell me,’ he snarled. ‘What have you done to Ella?’

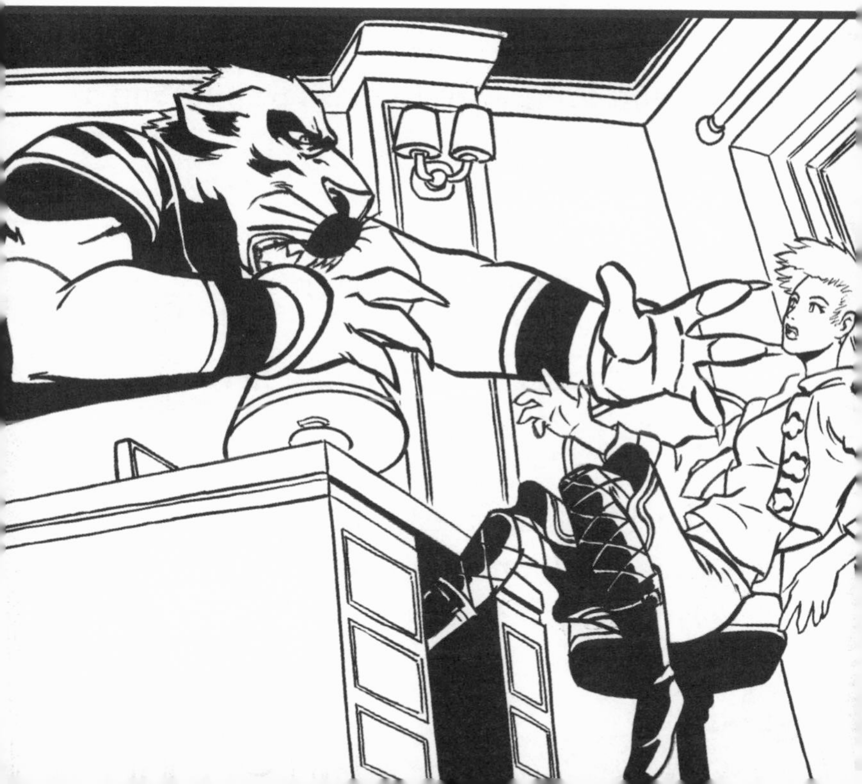

the
clonebot

Misha and Finn leapt forward to pull Suma off Ella, but just then the bedroom door opened and in came – Ella.

She was staring at Suma in amazement.

'Misha, what are you doing here? What's going on?'

The 'Ella' that Suma had jumped on lay silent on the floor. Although Suma had bitten deeply into it, there was no blood.

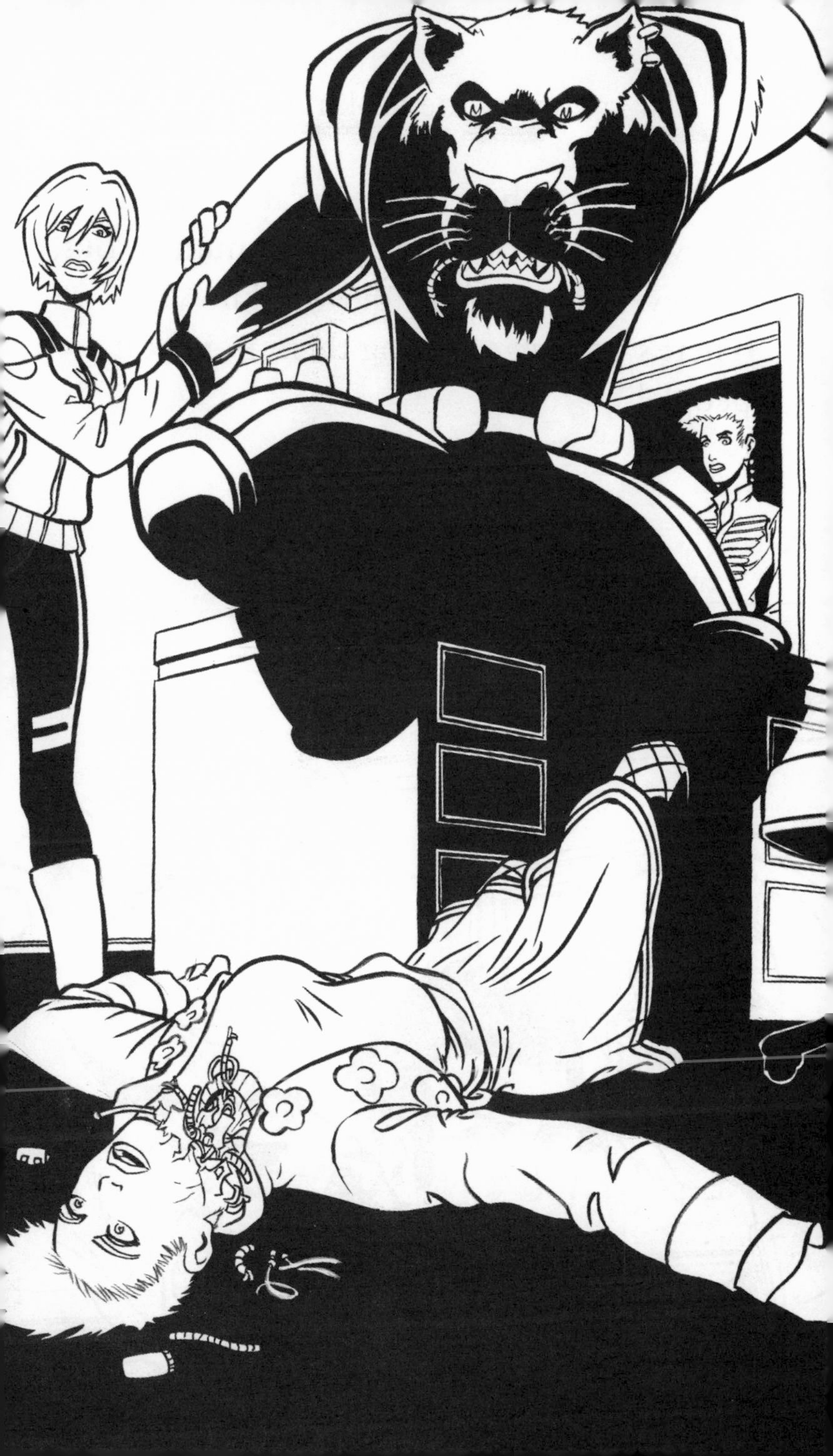

Ella saw everyone looking at it.

'It's a clonebot. It's identical to me in every way, but of course it's not human. But, whoever you are, how did you know? There's no way of telling them from real people!'

Suma's eyes flashed. This could look frightening – Misha and Finn knew it was his way of laughing. He said nothing.

'But Suma, why were you so angry?' asked Misha, changing the subject.

'How do we buy things? By looking into a machine that checks our eye patterns! The only way that this machine could do that … '

' … was if it had stolen my eyes!' laughed Ella. 'Well, as you see, my eyes are still in my head. Now, what are you doing here, and who are these guys?'

Misha went over to Ella and held her hand.

'We're the Starchasers, Ella. I've got some bad news. Your dad sent us to find you. I'm afraid – he's dying.'

Ella couldn't help herself. She sat down in the chair and started to roar with laughter.

ELLa's PLan

'Ella! Did you hear what I said? Your father is dying!'

'Is that what he told you? No he isn't, Misha. He'll live for years yet.'

'How do you know?'

'Because he's tried that one before. Look, Misha, and you Starchasers, whoever you are, sit down and listen. But promise me that you won't tell anyone else – that's for me to do.

'Making clonebots isn't allowed. If you can't tell them from real people, there are all sorts of ways you could use them for crime. But my father was determined to try. He made the first clonebot – and he made it look like me! It even had exactly the same eye pattern as I've got. Of course, it doesn't really think.'

'How does it work, then?'

'By remote control. You have to wear a virtual reality helmet. You can control everything the robot does or says. If the clonebot eats ice cream, you can even taste it!

'I knew my father was wrong to make one. I thought that if the government found out they would shut down the factory.'

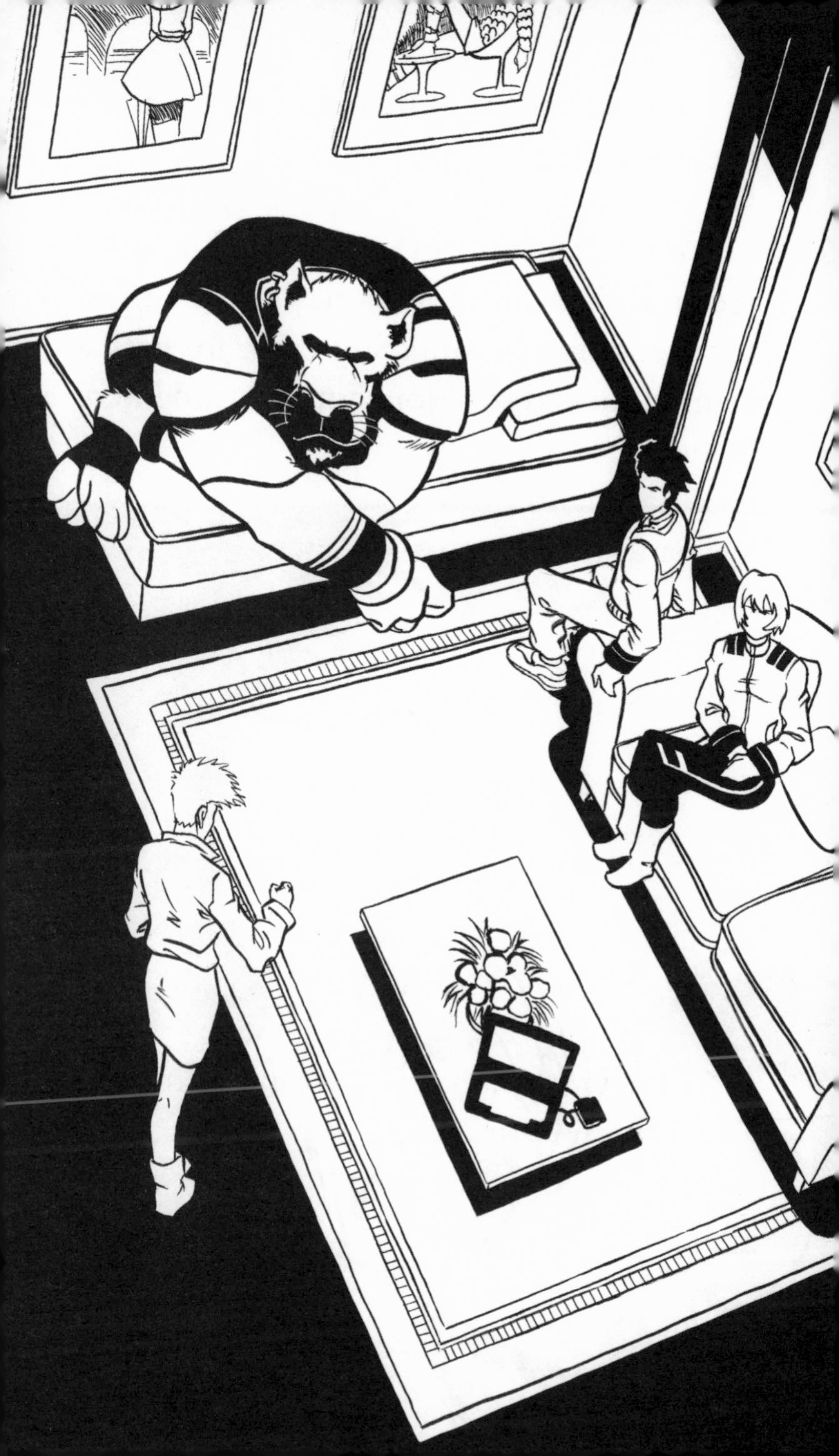

'So that was what the row was about!' said Finn.

'Yes – well, no, not exactly. Dad is really mean. He's got pots of money, but he hates me spending anything. So I came up with a plan. I pinched the clonebot and came here

to Trajan. I paid my hotel bill with cash so he couldn't track me. Then I used the robot to buy things.

'I can just imagine Dad's face when he got the bills. Of course, he can't say anything, otherwise I would go public on the clonebot!'

They all tried to imagine Ripp Gun's face when he got the bills. It wasn't that hard, because just at that moment the door opened and Ripp Gunn came in, looking about as cheerful as someone who's just had a huge bill for something he didn't want at all.

a bit
sneaky

Ella looked shocked.

'Dad! How did you find me?'

'The Starchasers are good! I knew they would find you. I followed them to this hotel, and bribed the porter to tell me your room number.'

'That porter's having a really great day,' muttered Finn.

'Now, Ella, you are coming home with
me. We've got some talking to do about
these bills.'

'Talking of bills,' said Misha, 'We've done
what you asked. How about paying our bill?'

'I've done it already. You can check your account if you like.'

Misha took out her spacephone and checked. The money was there, right enough.

'Thank you, Mister Gunn. Now we have the money perhaps we can talk about these illegal clonebots you have been making. I'm sure the galactic government would be very interested.'

Ripp Gunn didn't want to talk about them, but he could see he was going to have to.

'All right, but just remember this is top secret. I'm actually making them for the government!'

'Why?'

'Just think! Galaxy leaders aren't popular. Sometimes people try to kill them. It wouldn't matter if it was a clonebot! Some-

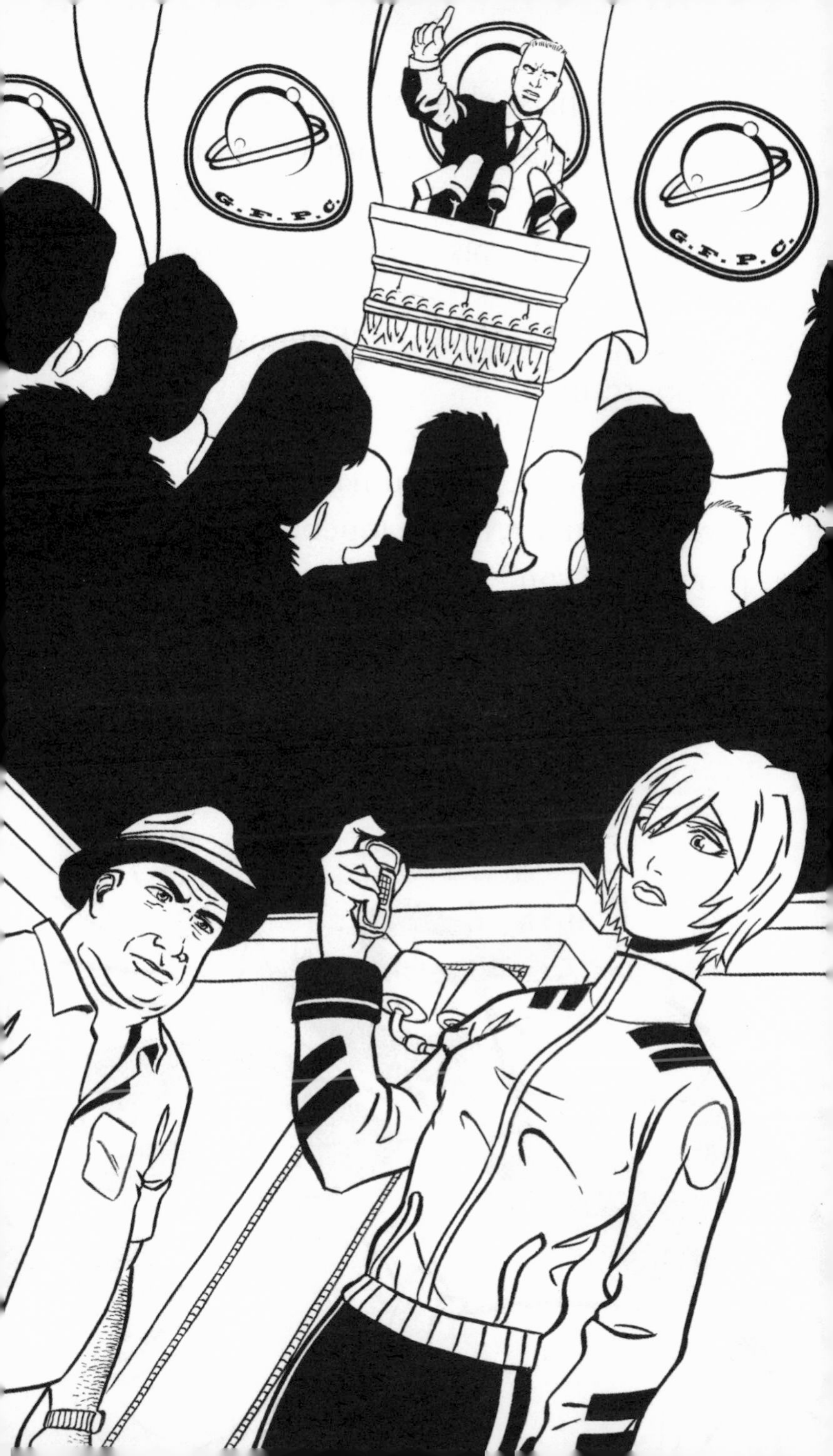
G.F.P.C.
G.F.P.C.

times they have to go to distant planets for meetings. Using a clonebot would mean they don't really have to go at all. No one would know it wasn't them!'

'Hmmm,' said Misha. 'Sounds a bit sneaky to me.'

'In any case,' said Suma. 'It won't work. I can tell humans from clonebots. And I can prove it to you.'

'Go, on prove it.'

'Easy. You're a clonebot.'

The clonebot showed Ripp Gunn's feelings really well.

'So all my work is wasted!'

'Well, maybe not,' said Suma. 'What's the deal if I can come up with a way to solve the problem?'

'Suma!' yelled Misha. 'You know that's a really bad idea!'

'Suma sighed. 'It's always the same. Every time I come up with a really good idea to make money … '

A week later, the Starchasers were back at base.

'So, Suma. How can you tell clonebots from humans? They looked pretty human to me!'

Suma just sat there, looking mysterious.

'Come on Suma, out with it!' ordered Misha.

'All right, but I'm not sure you'll want to hear this! You humans are good at lots things, but you don't have very good noses! If you did, you'd know that humans smell — a lot! — but clonebots don't smell of anything!'